Mind Map of Love is a novel by Christian Zott who in twenty-one chapters describes the various stages of a universal love story. At the end of many of the individual episodes – written in the form of trenchant short stories – there are turning points at which the reader him/herself can determine the future of the two main characters. This has created an original novel taking the form of a multifaceted kaleidoscope of love in eleven different variations.

Christian Zott is the founder and managing director of consultancy firm mSE Solutions GmbH with branches in Munich, Lübeck, Singapore and Pittsburgh. His company specialises in supply chain management and provides its services to customers throughout the world. In 2011 he took a break and it was during this time that the 'Mind Map of Love' project was born.

ᶜᶻbooks

Original title: "Mindmap der Liebe"
First edition in English 2014
CZ Books Verlag, Munich
Copyright © 2014 Christian Zott
This work is protected by copyright.
No part of this publication
may be reproduced, including extracts.

COVER
Mauro Fiorese

PHOTOGRAPHY
Christian Zott

LAYOUT
Hans-Joachim Ellerbrock

EDITED BY
Dr. Andreas Klement

ENGLISH TRANSLATION
Louisa Bird

PRINTING AND BINDING
tredition GmbH, Hamburg
Printed in Germany

ISBN 978-3-9816447-5-3

Mind Map of Love

A Novel by Christian Zott

To all seekers and lovers

TRUS[T]

ROMANTIC
LOVE

HOPEFUL
LOVE

TICKLE
LOVE

JEA[LOUS]

IN[

MIND MAP

OF LOVE

ETERNAL LOVE

FATE

DEATH

SURVIVING

DUTIFUL LOVE

NEW LOVE

HATE

VIOLENCE

DEPRESSION

SELF-LOVE

ISOLATED LOVE

REMORSE

LOVE FOR SALE

PENITENCE

SOLITUDE

Route Map

Preface

A small harbour on the Ligurian coast. Dancing on the sparkling waters are red and blue-painted fishing boats, returned from their morning fishing trips. An older fisherman is dragging an octopus of substantial size onto the quay wall. His young assistant is bringing a basket with freshly caught lobsters to shore. A beautiful woman, who has been waiting for him, receives him with a tender embrace. A white cat with red paws is tearing at a fish head someone has thrown for it. The waves are lapping gently against the breakwater; it smells of the sea and green algae.

Christian Zott is sitting in a small café on the piazza, observing the hustle and bustle. He is entirely in the here and now, taking in the colours and smells, observing the faces and expressions of the people in the square. He is enjoying the space to reflect on new topics and dream up new projects. One hundred and thirty-seven days of a long hike lie behind him, with many more ahead. His thoughts flow unfettered, instead of being focussed on searching for solutions.

As a young logistics expert of twenty-seven he founded a consultancy firm that recognised the changes and opportunities of a global economy at a very early stage. With offices in Munich, Lübeck, Singapore and Pittsburgh, the company has become an international group of companies operating worldwide. After spending twenty-five years building up and consolidating the company's position, Christian Zott allowed himself the freedom to tread new paths. His aim was to give himself the time and space for in-depth self-reflection and he wanted to redefine his role in the company by transferring more responsibility over to his employees. Extended periods of travel had often represented key points in his life, sometimes even turning points. These included trips to the solitude of the Canadian wilderness, to the Arctic ice of Greenland, or as now in Southern Europe.

Life's journey, life path, the road of life ... there are many expressions linking biographical development to movement. All these phrases associate life with a progression through the world in motion. It's almost as if life experiences are only made possible through movement.

A journey was also the trigger for this novel. Christian Zott undertook a five thousand kilometre hike across Southern Europe, almost forty kilometres a day, from its most westerly point in

Portugal to the Eastern border on the Bosporus. As a European through and through, his decision for this route was very deliberate. And he was not alone: the key works of European literature and philosophy on audio, from Homer and Aristotle to Dante and Goethe, were his trusty companions.

On his way along the coast he met a lot of people, and gradually noticed that they generally fell into one of two groups: „Seekers and lovers." This book is dedicated to them. He took photos with his smartphone, spontaneous snapshots along the route, and he soon realised that these pictures also focussed on the subject of „love", both literally and figuratively. Some of these photographs have been chosen for this book.

He begins to structure his thoughts, and attempts to assign a structure to this major emotion. To do this he employs a technique from psychology and management.

A mind map is used to open up a topic and to illustrate the key points. Transferred to literature, this method is the tool for describing the term ,love', which is often trivialised these days but which remains probably the most powerful of human feelings.

The book, developed during a journey, is an unusual reflection on the forms of love in our times. The particular way in which the novel was creation is reflected in various parts of the novel, most notably the settings. The twenty-one chapters take place in twenty different locations, mostly European cities but also pastoral scenescapes. These locations are never specifically named but are always clearly identifiable from characteristic details. Just as a traveller's overall mental recall of a trip becomes increasingly blurred as time passes, whereas individual memories such as a painting or the taste of a meal become increasingly prominent, the reader is guided through the locations in the novel via striking details.

Each of the individual chapters is written in the form of trenchant short story. Each of these episodes forms a potential point in a universal love story. The result is a kaleidoscope of love in its many manifestations, with the most beautiful and the ugliest, the most sincere and the lowest, the most animalistic and the most tender of emotions. It is no coincidence that the two protagonists are named after Shakespeare's famous romantic tragedy: Romeo and Juliet are simultaneously the happiest and most tragic couple.

At the end of many of the chapters, just as in an actual journey, there are turning points at which the reader can determine the course of the story. This creates eleven different stories or reading paths within one novel. This corresponds to a narrative style that is explicitly non-chronological. Our autobiographical memory often takes slightly bizarre routes; when we recall a particular event, a specific moment generally comes to mind first, from which we then reconstruct everything else. In the novel these processes of recall are simulated in the narrative, reflected in the fact that jumps in the timeframe in the shape of explanatory retrospectives or advance interpretations are a significant stylistic device in the novel.

Just as taking a long walk leaves the mind room for free associations, the individual episodes are structured by the sometimes fragmentary, sometimes hyper-realistic perceptions and memories of the narrator. And just as a journey shaped the origin and scope of this novel, travel itself becomes a key metaphor for the concept of love itself.

Andreas Klement

Hopeful Love

Above them the wooden propeller, inlaid with rattan, circled slowly and evenly. The flow of air provided a pleasant cooling sensation on her hot skin, dotted with small beads of sweat. Both doors to the balcony stood wide open, and the first rays of the morning sun were feeling their way into the room through the sheer curtain. From the streets came the hubbub of the dealers and a smell of roasted sesame rose up into the room.

It was still hot in the room from the day before and the heat of the impassioned night. She slept rolled up tightly on her side, an angelic smile on her face; he was lying on his back with open eyes, looking at the ceiling through the fan, reflecting on the crazy memories of the last few hours.

He had shivered as he walked along the pier, passing the rows of columns and watching the white fish in the clear black waters. „How can they even live here?", he thought, and gazed in amazement at the size of the old cistern that the Emperor Constantine had built centuries ago, a tranquil retreat under the lively, noisy city above it. He had come here early in the morning, virtually alone in the imposing complex, when he came upon the Gorgon heads upside down in the water in a rear section of the cistern, serving as bases to the columns.

The sight was disconcerting. Stairs led down to a small platform surrounded by a pool of water. In the middle stood a mighty Corinthian column

on a large stone block. The head of Medusa portrayed on the stone was turned upside down, the snake hair half in the water. It was not this sight that irritated him; it was her, with her red dress, her long black hair, trying in vain to perform a headstand. She fell over again and again, cursing. „Damn, can you please help me? I want to look Medusa straight in the eye! I want to find out what happens!" Baffled, he went over to her and helped her with her next attempt to stand on her head, supporting her with one hand, clasping her dainty ankles.

The two of them stood side by side like this for the first time, looking at the head of Medusa. Several minutes went by without a word being spoken. He glanced furtively at the flawless legs and black lace panties now showing from underneath her red dress as she stood on her head. He would later maintain that he had already fallen head over heels in love with her even before that point.

„Put me down again, I still haven't turned to stone, and anyway my head's exploding and it's cold. Let's go and have a drink. My name is Juliet." – „My name is Romeo."

Make a choice! Continue with ...
Romantic Love (p. 20) *or*
Fickle Love (p. 46)

Romantic Love

Romeo and Juliet had developed a remarkable skill over the years. Each was able to ascertain the desires of the other, even before they were uttered. They both made sparing use of this special gift to ensure that they remained at ease, without feeling oppressed with consideration for the other. They were both there for one another because each lived in balance. What had begun in a stormy fashion almost three years ago had become a solid unit with infinite space for both of them.

In late spring, the cracks were wide open and clear to see. Nevertheless, they had roped up and were moving slowly down the rear of the glacier with hearts beating fast, past craters, cracks and holes whose black openings appeared bottomless.

Romeo and Juliet had spent two years planning and saving to fulfil this dream, their first climbing tour together. Just two hours beforehand they had been sitting with their backpacks, ice picks, ropes and skis at a small station below the glacier and they waited with excitement for the train to take them to the summit. Their eyes were fixed on the huge north face of the Eiger. The sun cast sharp shadows against the mountain under the vast icefalls on the rock wall.

Romeo and Juliet were experienced mountain climbers, but surrounded by all these mighty peaks they both experienced a powerful sense of awe. The glacier shifted incessantly below them. They heard it cracking and saw more and more elongated fissures zigzagging through the blue ice brightly polished by the wind. Slowly they continued downwards, swing by swing, only the rope between them, their connection to life should one of them fall down a crevasse. Romeo went ahead, his thoughts with Juliet at all times. Juliet followed a rope length behind, her thoughts at all times with Romeo.

Finally they reached the big grey rock wall projecting vertically out of the ice, just as they had imagined it. The first rung of the iron ladder leading upwards was located high above them. The glacier was retreating year on year and the cabin at the top was accessed via a long metal staircase firmly anchored in the rock. Romeo climbed the first few metres across cold rock and secured Juliet on the first rung of the iron ladder. Slowly they climbed up to the cabin, crowning a small rocky plateau like an eagle's nest. They were alone, with no-one else in sight. The cabin was not serviced, and they wanted it that way.

The sun had heated the shingle wall of the cabin. Romeo and Juliet sat close together on their rucksacks, their backs pressed against the warm cabin wall. They didn't say a word for hours, gazing with fascination at the glacier. An ibex galloped across the ice to the next ledge on the opposite side of the glacial valley. „Do you see him?", asked Romeo. „Yes, how magnificent", Juliet replied. Romeo kissed Juliet tenderly on her lips chapped by snow and wind, stood up and began counting the rows of shingles on the cabin wall. „One, two, three rows up, then thirteen shingles to the right... Yes, it's moving!", muttered Romeo to himself, feeling a contentment and relief. He found the little box containing the ring for Juliet. He had been there the previous year and had concealed it until today, the big day.

Make a choice! Continue with ...
Trusting Love (p. 23) *or*
Dutiful Love (p. 31)

Trusting Love

Spring echoed up from downstairs. For the first time in two years they were all together again. All five children had come with their respective partners. Luisa had put the two small grandchildren to bed in a large basket placed on the top stone step of the theatre. Despite his many meetings, even her husband had made the journey.. He had landed about an hour ago and must have stubbornly squeezed through the crowds at the bottom to get up to the small, jovial group at the top. There were some 20,000 people in the theatre, sitting, standing or still looking for a space in the upper rows.

Luca, a friend of Romeo's, had pressed the ticket into Constantine's hand and smuggled him through the side entrance for the disabled. Naturally this was not entirely appropriate as Constantine was a bear of a man, almost two metres tall. Luca, on the other hand, merely used his good connections with the ladies on the entrance. He was a popular personality, having been born and raised here, and was quite the ladies' man. An Italian with plenty of heart and a passion for all beautiful things. Next to Luisa's basket they had spread out a blanket on which only Romeo and Juliet were sitting so far. The rest of the group were gazing in awe at the ancient amphitheatre built in the days of Emperor Tiberius. A fabulous setting for Vivaldi's Four Seasons. Juliet had curled herself up and was resting her head on Romeo's thighs. Her eyes shone and she was overwhelmed with happiness as she listened to the allegro of the first Violin Concerto.

Giunt'è la Primavera e testosetti
la salutan gl'augei con lieto canto,
e i fonti allo spirar de' zefferetti
*con dolce mormorio scorrono intanto.**

,Springtime returns and the birds
greet it with cheerful song
while a soft breeze caresses
the murmuring streams.'

Constanze, the youngest of the five siblings, had vehemently insisted on coming here, after the dramatic events of the past year and then spending an entire weekend together exploring the area. To drive to the lake, to go to that great restaurant at the old port, to bathe in the nearby spas and then to visit Dante on his column as a reminder as to how he, guided by Virgil, had proceeded through the inferno into paradise in search of his dead Beatrice. Juliet, however, was still alive!

In the early evening before the performance, Luca took them to a friend who ran a remarkably good restaurant close to the Piazza delle Erbe. His

friend's father welcomed them by cutting deliberately large helpings of various hams as a starter and placed the plates on the long table.

It was a loud, convivial dinner. Only the entrée interrupted the cheerful mood for a brief moment. The host's gift, a speciality of the farmer who supplied the lambs, was placed on the table. Two small pieces of something, reddish brown and bean-shaped, served on radicchio. Suddenly everyone was sitting frozen and quiet in front of their plates. Kidneys braised in Barolo sauce. – Romeo and Juliet were the first to burst out laughing and began to eat.

They had both been through hell the past year. The question was not whether or not Romeo wanted to be the donor; that was clear from the very first second. It was the time that passed so slowly before it was clear that the transplanted kidney had been accepted by Juliet's body.

* *La Primavera*, Antonio Vivaldi

Make a choice! Continue with ...
Eternal Love (p. 27) *or*
Fate (p. 37)

Eternal Love

The propellers made a dull sound and drew a long, foaming line across the flat blue sea. A school of dolphins played between the powerful waves at the bow and stern that grew apart from each other at an acute angle, extending virtually to the horizon. The sun fell, seemingly in slow motion, vertically into the sea. This was the moment Romeo and Juliet had been waiting for. Both had wanted for some time to experience the true equinox at this location. For the second time this year, day and night were of equal length and in a few minutes the sun would be directly over the equator. Back home, it was 23rd September, shortly after eleven o'clock in the morning; for these two lovers it was already six hours ahead

Romeo and Juliet had been lying wrapped in grey blankets for the whole afternoon, side by side on two sun-loungers. On each of the small tables right and left stood a glass of water. Romeo's walking frame was leaning in a little alcove on the stairway leading to the higher deck.

For a long time the two of them talked about their children at home, the many grandchildren who had kept them young, and they explored the countless memories of the past fifty years together. They giggled, occasionally cried, and finally reached a state of relaxed contentment. As so often, both allowed themselves to be inspired by the ideas of ancient and mod-

ern thinkers, and discussed Aristotle, Schopenhauer and Kant. They talked about what philosophy and religion tell us is to come. Is death really the end? Is death merely the stopover to a new life? Does death mean transitioning to a different state in the afterlife? „Whatever happens," Romeo said tenderly to his Juliet, „our essence will always be preserved". They drank a sip of water, Romeo sought Juliet's hand and they sat back to enjoy the blood-red spectacle of the setting sun. The night descended and very slowly their hands slid away from each other. Hours later, the stewardess from the Ocean Bar asked if she could bring them extra blankets.

Exactly one year before, Juliet had returned home with her research. As Romeo was no longer able to walk properly, she had to manage the household and organise their shared life alone. Despite everything, they were both content and experienced happy moments every day. In a long life together they had been able to experience many beautiful things. Juliet sat down with Romeo at the table and looked at him with soft, loving eyes. „Dearest, I have just a year, maybe two, to live". Speechless, Romeo took her hand and they spent a long time together in silence, inhabiting only the here and now.

The subsequent planning of the cruise turned out to be surprisingly easy. It was only the children and their partners, and even the grandchildren, who seemed intent on scuppering their plans. The pair had their work cut out persuading their offspring that they were not too old for a trip like this. And they requested that - should anything happen - their bodies were not to be brought home.

Achieving the true aim of their journey was decidedly more difficult, however. For one thing, Romeo was not as mobile as before, and for another, it was not easy to get in touch with the appropriate contacts. But one thing he had maintained throughout his entire life was an irrepressible desire to finish whatever he started once a decision had been made.

Romeo travelled by train to Switzerland to discuss all the issues for a dignified end to life. He had got the address from an old friend. The lady with whom he had already been in contact with for some time spoke calmly and sensitively. Time was short, and their journey was to begin in six months. All he needed was 30 grams of pentobarbital sodium, 15 grams for himself, 15 grams for Juliet.

Dutiful Love

Romeo's accident had happened over 15 years ago now. He sat in his wheelchair, the large oak desk at his back, in front of his wide office windows. From the thirtieth floor, Romeo had a fabulous view of the aircraft landing at the nearby airport. He couldn't remember a time before all the buildings and the ongoing construction works. What had once been a compact airport had become a voracious giant striding over long distances. He had to fly though, so for Romeo it was a blessing in disguise. His high social status and disability both meant that he was always picked up by a chauffeur and taken directly to the plane ahead of the queues.

He loved this view from his office, especially at dawn when a sentimental yearning for far-away destinations awoke in him. Sometimes he wished he could simply fly away to some other distant place.

Romeo turned his wheelchair 180 degrees with some skill, rolled back to his workstation and answered the final few emails for the day. In half an hour his father-in-law would be round for their daily meeting, but first he wanted to speak to his assistant about plans for the following day. He was expecting business partners from Asia and Canada, and he was double-booked. No-one would be at work tomorrow to answer the phone calls. But it was impossible to change anything and, in any case, he had managed to overcome every tricky situation that had presented itself so far.

At eight o'clock on the dot, Pa was standing in the doorway asking the obligatory question as to whether or not Romeo minded if he smoked his cigar in his office. Naturally he didn't; it was for precisely this reason that Romeo had removed the smoke detectors and sprinkler system. The insurance firm were charging a fortune to keep the entire building contractually insured despite this exception. Pa, Juliet's father, had taken over the private bank from his father and expanded it into a very successful company. He had just one daughter, and in his very conservative view, Romeo was a man and should therefore be the one to take his place in the business.

Then the terrible accident occurred. Even though Romeo had been able to push Juliet out of the road and save her, he had been hit by the drunken truck driver instead, and was seriously injured. Pa sat by his side for days in the hospital. It was then that he had decided that whatever happened, he would train Romeo up and entrust the bank to him one day. Two months later, he insisted on personally collecting Romeo from the hospital. Pa had bought a car that was specially customised, Romeo's first company car, with which he was able to drive himself home despite his disability.

For a long time Romeo and Juliet wanted to remain free and independent. Ever since Romeo had met her, Juliet had fought tooth and nail against being perceived as the daughter of one of the country's most successful businessmen. She wanted to achieve everything on her own. From financing her studies to life with Romeo, which she wanted to lead simply and without extravagance. Everything was different now. They were no longer able to continue their climbing activities in the mountains together and Juliet did not want to pursue her hobby alone. She wanted to be there for Romeo at all times, even during the day when he was concentrating on his work. He had saved her life. Her life now belonged to him.

During those years, Romeo had undergone a personal training programme with the best private banker in the country. He was an able pupil and soon became an internationally respected senior manager. At the same time, Romeo took a teaching position at the local university, and had to turn down a position as visiting professor at the University of Hong Kong because the travel time was incompatible with his existing duties.

Over time, Romeo accepted his fate and became a new person. Whilst his and Juliet's goals before the terrible event had been freedom, the outdoor life, a large family of their own and a job working for a sports goods manufacturer, their lives had now changed completely. After Romeo's accident they could no longer have children of their own, and Juliet waited day after day in a large villa with staff, until he was brought home by his driver. Romeo had only one goal: to become one of the best in his sector.

And so the love between them changed. They both needed each other. Juliet needed Romeo, to whom she felt obliged. Romeo needed Pa, who had given him a leg-up in his career. And he needed Juliet, who had graciously dedicated her life to being there for him, always.

Fate

Juliet trembled, holding Romeo's head in her lap as she brushed aside the sticky hair from his face. She screamed hysterically, his severed body laying beside her.

If the restaurant at the Placa de les Olles hadn't been closed, they certainly would have been sitting at that amazing, long bar. Everything at that place was freshly prepared in front of the guests: Pimientos, Almejas, Bonito, Anchoas, Chipirones, Navajas, Pata Negra... . Juliet knew Romeo well enough to know that there would be a second bottle of Macabeu Penedès on the table. But it was the weekend and the restaurant was not open.

Instead, they had stood for a long time in front of the huge, unfinished basilica, whose gates symbolised the virtues of hope, faith and love. The architect's idiosyncratic style, at first glance inspired by something incomprehensible, held Romeo and Juliet captivated. Sprawling symbolism flooded their senses with impressions that were elusive and not immediately open to interpretation. The longer their eyes glided across the huge façade, the more details they discovered.

Many years had passed since their first encounter in the old cistern in that city on the Bosporus strait. They had led a happy life. Although they were not particularly wealthy, they had always had enough. Every year they treated themselves to a weekend to dive in and explore the history of a city, define themselves in the present and decide together the next steps.

The most important thing holding them back was always the family that had grown significantly in recent years. All five children were now married and had provided them with many grandchildren. The feeling of unity within the extended family was strong and everyone spent a considerable amount of time together. Whenever possible Romeo and Juliet spent a lot of time outdoors, cycling, walking in the mountains or in their small sailing boat at one of the lakes nearby. This kept them fit and healthy and, aside from Juliet's kidney failure ten years ago, they were both in good health. Here they now were, standing up straight, humble and grateful side by side, hand in hand in front of this magnificent basilica.

As Romeo wanted to see the city from up high, they were on their way to the small hilltop excursion point, not far from the city centre. The pair waited for the Tramvia Blau, the historic tram that would take them to the top. Stretching out behind them was a wonderful view of the Hotel Metropolitan, known as La Rotonda, built in a modernist style which Romeo photographed with fascination.

Even though the old tram only had a top speed of 6 miles an hour, the guard was unable to respond quickly enough. The tram entered the station almost silently, precisely at the moment when Romeo, taking pictures at the edge of the platform, toppled backwards and fell onto the tracks. The right carriage wheel made such a clean cut that the passengers inside the carriage did not even notice a thing.

Make a choice! Continue with ...
Death (p. 39) *or*
Surviving (p. 42)

Death

The gentle breeze coming from the north-east was favourable, and once the anchor had been lifted, it would propel her small sailboat back to port. Juliet had long been waiting for the right day. It was a warm, clear night and reflections of the stars sparkled on the dark lake. And in amongst all the stars, she imagined he would appear above her and have a clear view of her below.

He jests at scars that never felt a wound.*

The small boat had been bobbing about for quite a while, not too far from the shore. A moment ago, as dusk was falling, Juliet could clearly make out the cross in the lake in front of the castle, marking the spot where King Ludwig II had drowned. Now the darkness had swallowed both.

By the light of her headlamp, Juliet read the last few pages of Albert Camus' essay, Le Mythe de Sisyphus. The idea of overcoming the futility of one's own existence by defiant acceptance of tragedy and duty had occupied her thoughts constantly since the terrible event a year ago.

To love a person means to agree to grow old with them.** Did the reverse also hold true: that to lose a loved one means to agree to follow them? Juliet fought in vain against the confusion of her thoughts. Naturally,

the whole family had been trying to support her. She had even sought help from various therapists, who told her that she had to learn to love herself if she wanted to overcome the grief. All in vain.

That afternoon, Juliet had rigged up their shared sailboat alone for the first time. She contented herself with the small head sail, for she was in no hurry. Now she sat motionless in the boat, the book folded on her lap, and watched the cement hardening. She had mixed it at home and placed it on board in a bucket. As she sank both her feet into it, small air bubbles rose up, tingling against the soles of her feet, and the mixture warmed up. Juliet was glad, as her feet were normally cold.

Slowly, she pulled up the anchor and lifted it gently into the boat. With significant effort, she sat down on the small platform at the stern of the boat and dragged her legs, anchored in the bucket, over the side. She sat like this for a few minutes, looked up to her star, then gave herself a little push. Juliet clearly felt when the weight at her feet touched the bottom of the lake. It was a quiet death.

* *Romeo & Juliet,* Act 2, Scene 2,
William Shakespeare

** *Myth of Sisyphus*, Albert Camus

Surviving

From the speakers, Bach's *Orchestral Suite No. 3* boomed out in competition with the crashing waves and the storm that simply wouldn't let up. It was as if Odysseus' companions had just opened the leather bag that had imprisoned all the winds.

It was already getting light when Luca finally rounded the northernmost section of the archipelago surrounded by water. For hours he had been sailing against the wind to the north, to catch the right moment. Then suddenly, before he knew it, it was already time. Up on the top of the mountain an invisible force hurled high fountains of magma from the interior far up into the night sky, flowing into thin streams of lava over the crater and adorning the ridge like ruffled strands of hair.

The spectacle of nature high up on the volcano was just as stirring as the scene at the bottom on the sailing ship. The Tyrrhenian sea was churning and Juliet clung to the rail while Luca fought against the wind with each wave. He had succeeded in doing what he had promised her days before in the small island harbour:

„I'll take you to the limits of Hades, then you can talk to him again and say goodbye for your journey thereafter. Yes, but don't do the same as Orpheus, take your leave and live!" Smiling through her tears*, she agreed.

Romeo's sudden death had taken Juliet captive. For weeks she walked absent-mindedly through all the rooms in the house, round and round, and when she reached the last room, she returned to the first; and so it went on. When she could no longer bear it, she meandered through the city. But even on her aimless wanderings she could not shake the memories. Like a slideshow without a stop button, the images moved across her mind's eye without end. Despite professional help and support from her family, her life was out of control, and a longing for death was her constant companion.

Then, suddenly, Luca appeared. All at once he was standing before Juliet in the little chapel where she had lit hundreds of candles of remembrance. Luisa had driven there herself to deliver Luca for what she confided in him was going to be a last ditch attempt to save Juliet. It had taken weeks for Juliet to consent. He had tried to reassure her that she could get back off the boat again at any port. But Luca's plan inspired her and she was adamant that Romeo had whispered to her the previous night: „Do it, Juliet!"

Luca was fulfilling a long-cherished dream with this trip. For years he had been building his own boat which he wanted to sail across the Mediterranean from East to West and back again to a small Greek island. It was to be a journey in the footsteps of Ulysses, with a copy of Homer's epic on board at all times to scan the verses for any insights into currents, shorelines and settings for these mythical tales. „We're simply reversing the story", said Luca, „and this time Penelope is on board."

They sailed back to the island they had left that morning. The sea was still rough, with strong winds, and the boat rolled with every wave. But in the midst of the churning ocean, Juliet felt a deep calm spreading within her. Slowly the glow of the mountain faded into the darkness and for Juliet, it was like bidding farewell to a wonderful period in her life. She could already see the beacon of the small harbour in the distance and for a long time she once more felt anticipation for what the future held.

* *The Iliad*, Book VI, Homer

Fickle Love

He just couldn't leave her alone when she put on her makeup. He also loved it when she went out without any underwear, wearing nothing underneath her evening dress. For over two years they had enjoyed unbridled sex; anywhere, any place, any time.

Juliet stood bent forward at the sink, her face very close to the mirror, and wore dark lipstick to match her smoky eyes. Romeo was standing behind her, looking at her heavenly back revealed by the low-cut dress, and very slowly penetrated her. It was the evening after their arrival in this wonderful old town. They both came together, silently.

Romeo and Juliet were standing on the terrace gazing out over the rooftops of the Eternal City and looking forward to dinner together. The chef held numerous awards, the highest being the third Michelin star for his restaurant which he had received a few years ago.

It was a breathtaking to be able to gaze upwards at over 2000 years of history. The pair also often found the metropoles of Shanghai, Hong Kong or

Singapore stunning when viewed from one of the city hotspots. But here it was different. The night was clear, lit with stars, and smelled of citrus. San Pietro, Castel Sant'Angelo, the Tiber, the Pantheon, Piazza Navona, the Colosseum, the Field of Mars... everything was within reach. At that moment they felt very close to one another, but each remained their own person.

Romeo had reserved the third table by the window with a direct view of the self-supporting dome of the Duomo. As ever, Juliet was drinking a glass of 1996 Dom Pérignon Rosé. Romeo did not like champagne; on occasions like this he ordered a Henri Bardouin Pastis, water and the ice on the side. He loved to mix it himself.

The next three hours were a feast! They started with salmon-basse marinated in yuzu and lemongrass, followed by baked courgette flowers with caviar in a crustacean and saffron consommé, continuing with spaghettini with scorpionfish, tomatoes and peppers, followed by a variation of duck on Jerusalem artichoke purée, finishing with a selection of the finest cheeses. As accompaniments they drank a bottle of Pouilly Fumé Silex 2010 from Didier Dagueneau's legendary estate and a bottle of 1999 Chambolle-Musigny.

Romeo and Juliet were in high spirits and it could have been a perfect evening. Juliet gushed about her purchases at Hermès, Valentino and Gucci. Romeo exuberantly recounted his impressions of Michelangelo's

unique representation of the Last Judgement in the Sistine Chapel. Neither of them was really listening to the other, and they might just as well have been talking to themselves about their own desires and pleasures; the other person was just an accessory. It didn't bother either of them, however; their lives were good and free from financial burden.

But then, at the end of this extraordinary evening, it was only a small thing – perhaps a moment of thoughtlessness – that was to instantly destroy all the beauty and intimacy between them, bursting the bubble of happiness and expectation. They had reached the final course and Juliet slowly and pleasurably drew the cheese knife across her mouth to enjoy the final few morsels of the excellent Epoisses. Her eyes were closed as she did so.

To Romeo, this vulgar gesture had something warrior-like about it and was altogether quite unsavoury. Following this single action, the whole raft of emotions that had built up in him came crashing down. He simply couldn't reconcile the sight of Juliet's angelic face with the cheese knife in her mouth. Later on, asleep, he had nightmares in which Juliet sat before him with the laughing grimace of The Joker.

Make a choice! Continue with ...
Jealousy (p. 50) *or*
Infidelity (p. 83)

Jealousy

On a stormy night of love, during the waves of a seemingly endless orgasm, Juliet bit Romeo's bottom so hard that his leg was numb for days afterwards, right down to his toes. The wound was so severe that they both had to think long and hard about whether or not they should actually go to a hospital emergency room. But it was Good Friday in a predominantly Catholic city and so they decided to stop the bleeding themselves to avoid the embarrassing situation of having to explain what had happened. Romeo clenched his buttocks and Juliet sat down on him, eating crackers, with a gauze bandage as a compress between their buttocks. Since they could barely move for the next few hours, they watched one of their favourite films: *Fight Club* by David Fincher.

A few weeks later, once the bruise had shimmered in all the colours of the rainbow and followed gravity to travel down his thigh, the result of Juliet's bite displayed exceptional beauty. A scar had formed over the once gaping wound and bore a striking resemblance to the zig-zag tattoo underneath the right eye of tattoo artist Kat Von D. The symbol suited Romeo's muscular rear end rather well. Juliet was proud of her masterpiece and, after some time, Romeo came to terms with it too.

Juliet went to this bar a few steps away from the court garden on an almost daily basis. In a single, elegant move, an older, very attractive man with silvery white, wavy hair slid a coaster down the bar for the glass of champagne in front of Juliet. Instead of beer mats that would have looked rather coarse in this establishment, the owner used coasters made of absorbent white paper and changed the motifs printed on them regularly. For that reason, Juliet didn't immediately notice the latest picture,  but then it hit her like a lightning bolt; she clearly recognised Romeo's rump!

Only a few months ago a woman had discovered Romeo's bite scar as they were both relaxing in the sauna of their favourite spa hotel. Later on in the hotel bar, it turned out that the „stupid cow", as Juliet called her, was an advertising photographer who not would not take no for an answer until she had persuaded Romeo into some photographs as a „model with a bite". Ever since then, Romeo had been spending the little free time that remained available to him outside of his punishing work schedule constantly on the go with this woman to have his famous rear photographed in the most beautiful places in the world.

On every advertising column, in every fashion magazine and now even on the coaster at her favourite bar, Romeo's rump with her bite mark was simply everywhere. Juliet could barely take it anymore; it felt like running the gauntlet. The hypocritical, spiteful and duplicitous remarks from her friends were becoming more and more intolerable by the day.

She was increasingly tormented by torturous jealousy towards this blonde photographer who was taking Romeo away from her a little at a time. A hitherto unknown feeling was taking over Juliet. Was it the fear of loss, or existential angst? Maybe it was even simply the irrational idea of being cheated on in public.

Make a choice! Continue with ...
Hate (p. 54) *or*
Depression (p. 71)

Hate

Juliet was feeling increasingly troubled. Ever since Romeo had achieved international success, she was tormented by an indefinite jealousy. Was he cheating on her? If Juliet was truly honest with herself, it was not a potential affair that was her real concern. Her ugly antipathy towards Romeo originated more from a rather unsavoury emotional cocktail of wounded vanity, envy and fear of losing face.

Her feelings were constantly changing between a kind of love – or at least affection – for Romeo and then, a moment later, bitter aversion and contempt. Juliet's mental state was deteriorating dramatically. She hadn't left the house for weeks. The staff, from the maid to the gardener, seemed to be forever whispering behind her back. Soon she had convinced herself beyond all doubt that they all knew something that she only suspected.

Juliet finally found what she was looking for online: the agency promised 24-hour surveillance with a worldwide network of specialists able to obtain evidence using the latest technology. The company even gave a guarantee of success for achieving the desired result. Should Romeo fail to slip up during the week-long monitoring period, a proactive approach was also available for considerable additional cost, naturally. In these cases, the agency delivered „attractive bait" to subject the husband to a „tough test". There were detailed questionnaires on the company's website to ensure that the „bait" corresponded as closely as possible to the target's ideal.

All in all, this service was exactly what Juliet was looking for to keep her ever burning hatred of Romeo in check. The only problem was the price. The agency was extremely expensive and the quote was a high, five-figure sum, even excluding the cost of the seduction test. But Juliet's heart was so filled with hate that she laid the blame for the situation fully at Romeo's door and intended to make him pay for his own surveillance. As Romeo had always generously left her his credit and debit cards, Juliet transferred across an eighty percent downpayment, and the agency began its work.

Every evening at six o' clock Juliet paced around the rooms in their shared house in almost hysterical expectation of the daily report from the project manager. It was the fourth day and nothing had happened! Although Romeo was always at photo shoots and at night he was the star with all the hip party people, he went to bed alone every time, and his only phone calls were with his company and his wife.

Juliet was seething with fury and quarrelled with herself: „Dammit! Am I making a complete fool of myself here?" She just couldn't admit defeat

this time. Was everything she had borne in recent times – from love to jealousy and hatred – simply a figment of her imagination? She didn't want to admit this, and she just couldn't accept it.

And what was scheduled to happen, happened. The next day an exotic beauty with chocolate brown skin, slender as a gazelle, attended the hotel gym seemingly at random at exactly the moment Romeo was finishing up his morning workout.

Make a choice! Continue with ...
New Love (p. 58) *or*
Violence (p. 64)

New Love

Juliet lived alone; she had separated from Romeo some time ago. Even though Romeo had constantly professed his love for her and claimed never to have cheated on her, Juliet did not believe him. Her pride was so badly hurt that she eventually broke up with him; she simply didn't want to go on any longer. Her decision was also fuelled by the opinions of her sister, her duplicitous friends (generally men with ulterior motives) and especially her mother and they all said Juliet must be in the right.

After the divorce was hastily finalised and she achieved the freedom she had chosen for herself, Juliet started going out on the town. Almost every day she got herself slightly drunk and ready to party her nights away in the city's clubs. But after a year of this, she had to concede that the men who spent night after night in these places in the hope of getting lucky just weren't all that impressive in the cold light of day. Juliet then registered with a number of online services. These promised to quickly find you your ideal life partner. During this phase, Juliet's habits changed drastically. Her friends were amazed that she was no longer to be found on the slopes, and they jokingly threatened to submit a missing person's report.

Juliet had been living in a whole different world, however. The addiction to finding her new life partner via these dating sites occupied all of her time. She was continuously answering the many offers that came in but

she found it difficult to assess their seriousness. Soon she started creating categories and classifying these strangers and their pseudonyms into „pervert", „sex addict", „one night stand", „frustrated", „poser", „coward" and „sincere seeker". For a long time she couldn't find anyone to fit that last category.

Until one day someone called Don_Juan_111 wrote to her. The number at the end of his online identity did rather suggest that there were plenty of other men on the Net using the same pseudonym, but what this Don_Juan_111 wrote moved Juliet deeply. His sentences were wonderfully formulated, as well as free of errors, which distinguished him from the majority of the other candidates. Even more remarkable than his writing style were the subjects he covered. He switched skilfully between stories about himself to the dreams that excited him. He wrote about how immoderate indulgence in life's pleasures could lead you astray, of egoism, modesty and transience, and how to balance out such problems with reflection and insight. Juliet had the impression that he was talking about things that he himself had experienced as well as about desires that as yet remained unfulfilled. He wrote and Juliet answered – following her true feelings for the first time – with no game-playing or ulterior motives.

Every message from Don_Juan_111 moved Juliet, and made her heart beat with excitement. She didn't understand how anonymous lines from a stranger could stir up so many feelings. Almost every night she asked herself, „Is it his well-chosen words or his moving sentences that keep my attention, or is it my imagination running away with me to think that I may be a little closer to a new happiness?"

Juliet and Don_Juan_111 had exchanged intriguing letters for over six months, but neither had the courage to arrange a meeting. Both were waiting eagerly for the other to make the first move. Their words danced coquettishly around the question of how it would be to move things from the virtual to the real world. But day after day they delayed addressing that issue, even though every night before they went to sleep each wished for another message to be waiting in their mailbox when they awoke.

When Juliet's curiosity finally got the better of her and she was no longer able to resist coming out of the shadows, she plucked up the courage and wrote: „We need to meet, Don Juan!" She deliberately avoided the „111" part. Don Juan replied immediately with just one sentence: „Juliet, it is not only love that is the true essence of life*, it is also hope that keeps us alive." And so she agreed on a date for the long-awaited first meeting.

Don Juan had left a plane ticket at the Iberia desk for Juliet, along with a letter. He had said goodbye to his old life years ago, he wrote, and was now living in a new place. He gave her the address of his favourite bar where he would be waiting for her that evening with a red rose.

Juliet sat on the plane, hands clammy with excitement, and thought once again about the situation she now found herself in. There was still time, she could take the next plane straight back home. But her yearning heart would not permit it.

She almost got lost in the maze of narrow streets of the picturesque district of Santa Cruz, before she finally found herself standing in front of the bodega. A mix of rough, loud voices reached the outside through the open door. Juliet almost turned tail and fled, but she summoned all her courage and pushed her way into the narrow tapas bar, past the crowded tables and busy waitresses to search desperately for a man with a rose. People at the bar were standing two deep but Juliet still managed to spot a small red rose on the counter. The man in question was sitting with his back to her on a bar stool and was chatting animatedly with the bartender. Juliet squeezed between two gesticulating men and tapped the stranger on the shoulder. Don Juan stood up and as he turned around, both froze. Standing in front of Juliet was Romeo.

* adapted from *Faust I*, Johann Wolfgang von Goethe

Violence

What was truth, what were lies? What was wrong, what was right? Juliet concealed herself from reality behind the mask of her egocentricity. Why couldn't the world be as she wanted it to be? She felt she had the right to that, as she had seen herself as a victim her entire life. Ever since childhood she had felt unloved and had been running away from herself. As a young person she had always laid the responsibility for what happened to her in life firmly at the feet of circumstances around her. Nevertheless, she gave much of herself in relationships, not really out of love but more with the intention of achieving her own goals. But these goals were blurred and intangible for Romeo and for herself. So she clung to almost everyone she met during the course of her life. The opinions of others shaped her arguments even though they were often contradictory. She adjusted her behaviour to please the people she followed on her haphazard course, in both her appearance and her ways of thinking.

How could it be that even this extremely attractive dark-skinned woman had failed to seduce Romeo? Juliet was convinced that he had got wind of the surveillance and was therefore pretending to be a well-behaved, loyal husband. She had to get to the bottom of this mysterious affair as quickly as possible, because she couldn't be wrong!

The young woman, called Ambra, was half African. Her mother had been forced to swim the last few metres to Lampedusa after the overcrowded refugee boat capsized in the surging waves. A young Italian who was just complet-

ing his military service on the island pulled her out of the water. The two later married and lived in Campania where Ambra – protected by four brothers – grew up in a city dominated by the camorra, the local crime syndicate.

Juliet met Ambra in a charming village on the Ligurian coast between Genoa and the Cinque Terre. They sat on the terrace in the morning sun and drank cappuccino, but Juliet barely glanced at the beautiful view of the harbour below. „How come you didn't manage to get him into bed?", Juliet asked bluntly.

Ambra reported on her meeting with Romeo, how she was readily asked to come along to his shoots and invited to attend the parties afterwards. But she was just one of many who showed an interest in Romeo so it wasn't easy to achieve Juliet's objective. In any case, aside from the odd meaningless bit of flirting with one beautiful woman or another, Romeo always remained on his own. He left every party alone, and the video surveillance secretly installed in his hotel room only confirmed his loyalty. At that moment Juliet wanted to draw a line under the whole saga but, as so often happened in life, things turned out rather differently.

After the business part of the meeting was over, Ambra became more relaxed and talked about her big brother, Carlos, who worked on one of the small islands not far off the coast at a winery and who had even been promoted to cellarman. A meal and wine tasting was held on the island once a month. For Ambra's brother it was the last event of this kind before he was due to leave the island a few weeks later.

Carlos had brutally stabbed Ambra's first boyfriend when he had discovered the boyfriend had got a little too close to his sister. After a short trial, he was sent to this small island's prison and was selected for a rehabilitation programme. The prison management worked with a renowned wine producer and ran a vineyard there. Under the guidance of experienced winemakers, the prisoners produced a very drinkable drop of wine. When Juliet heard the story she instantly became excited and so the two ladies made their way to catch the boat destined for the island the next morning along with the other invited guests.

Carlos had really gone all out on his appearance for his farewell party from the island. Around his neck on a chain hung a spittoon designed specially for the institution in recognition of the fine art of winemaking, decorated with two small silver handcuffs to symbolise his training at this special place. The convicts had received the group of visitors from the mainland and accompanied them during this culinary event; now Carlos was sitting at the table with his sister and Juliet. They talked animatedly about life in prison and the viticulture programme that had opened up whole new perspectives for its participants.

From the very first second, Juliet was fascinated by Carlos. It was not simply his mighty appearance that captivated her, it was his manner, the way he could speak and listen at the same time. She couldn't imagine how this pleasant man had been capable of such an atrocity. Was his criminal potential just waiting to come out again, or had his time on the prison island and the meaningful work really made a different man of him? Was it possible to change one's character permanently, or did people learn here how to recognise their dark side and control it?

Later, Juliet talked about her unhappy childhood and her life with Romeo who had hurt her so deeply and driven her to the brink of insanity. Carlos hung on her every word, and even a blind man could see just how passionate his interest in her was. It was on this evening that the spark was lit between Juliet and Carlos. Before the two women returned to the boat going back to the mainland, Carlos bade them farewell with a gift of the wine he had produced himself.

A few days later Juliet was back in the small harbour waiting for the boat with Carlos, who had been liberated from the prison island. Juliet had booked a hotel room where they went immediately after Carlos' arrival. There they experienced their first stormy night of love. Until the early hours of the morning, Juliet was in Carlos' strong arms and spoke again and again of her sadness caused by the hated Romeo who had destroyed her life. But now she had finally found her place in the world, she told Carlos, and she was happy. They had already made plans for the future and intended to run a vineyard together in Campania. He was to make the wine, she was to sell it. Juliet could even visualise the label for their wine bottles.

There was just one thing he wanted to take care of, and in his eyes Juliet could see his icy determination. At this moment the old instincts of protection were rising up again in Carlos. His former pattern was still active.

Days later the homicide squad examined a body that had been strangled with a thick wire, normally used in the cultivation of vines. The corpse was lying on its stomach, hands tied behind the back. The noose around the head was connected to the ankles, the legs were bent. The man had vainly struggled against death as long as possible by hollowing his back and pushing his legs upwards. But as his muscles began to tremble and he could no longer hold his legs, he had strangled himself in a slow and agonising death. A tried and tested method of organized crime in southern Europe. The police department was faced with a puzzle.

Depression

Compulsive trains of thought repeated themselves in Juliet's head over and over, but she couldn't help herself. Romeo was no longer there; she had driven him away herself. It was not what she wanted, but she had to do it. She no longer trusted him, but at the same time, did not know why. There was no specific reason; she was guided by sinister feelings. Her suspicions were followed by desperation, from a persistent sadness grew fear, and fear became loneliness.

Every morning Juliet woke up a broken woman, her reason and emotions in conflict. Until late in the evening she just lay there, tormented by tangled thoughts, and often she didn't sleep all night. She was exhausted and no longer saw any point in battling through the dark days. Hateful thoughts were eating away at any joy she might experience like piranhas; she could no longer summon up any happy feelings. She was on her own once more, but after her relationship with Romeo, being alone was unbearable.

Juliet wanted to run away from herself and, as she did every year for New Year's Eve, she travelled to the hotel where she had previously always been with Romeo. All afternoon she sat on the terrace, staring across the frozen lake to the other side of the valley to the Piz Rosatsch mountain. Finally, she went to her room.

There were figures on the wall, moving slowly. From time to time they merged, only to sepa-

rate again a moment later. The ticking of the clock on the antique chest of drawers next to the bed was a dull sound in the dark and silent solitude of the room.

Tick, tick, tick, tick... The dark shapes on the wall moved jerkily. Penetrating the old wooden door were voices from a joy-filled party, becoming ever louder. Shadows were visible at the bottom crack in the door where a thin strip of light shone into the room. There were four of them, the voices grew fainter, faded and ceased abruptly when the elevator door closed.

Tick, tick, tick, tick... The shadows appeared back on the wall and fought with a unicorn that disappeared suddenly. Was it tomorrow already or still yesterday? The pale moonlight highlighted ice crystals on the windows, divided up by bars. The crystals looked like stars that had fallen from the sky, prevented from entering the room by the window panes.

Tick, tick, tick, tick... Another burst of voices, someone looking for their shoe, giggles, the sound of glass shattering, and then silence. On top of the chest of drawers galloped a lone rider; the girl at the base of the table lamp sat there, filled with sadness, and cried. It was cold under the warm blanket. The elevator door opened again, a clatter of heels, a shadow swept by, a door slammed and, once more, the silence returned.

Dull firecrackers sounded in her ears as if through cotton wool, the stars on the windows were now colourful, flashing all shades of the rainbow and displacing the dark figures on the wall. Light, dark, light, dark. Later, she heard the ticking again, only further away and quieter on the threshold of eternity*.

The elevator door opened, voices talking at once, shadows came and glided quickly by. Was it time to get up already? Was a new year about to start? No, everything was still dark, the shadows returned. Finally, her eyelids became heavy, day came, and Juliet slept.

* Title of a painting by Vincent Van Gogh painted in 1890

Make a choice! Continue with ...
Self-love (p. 75) *or*
Isolated Love (p. 79)

Self-love

The large rose window above the triple portal took her breath away. The Gothic cathedral reminded her of magnificent French buildings more than any other church she had seen on her journey so far. Juliet was sitting at a round table in front of a café with a well-deserved glass of vino blanco in front of her. She had covered her allotted distance for today, and tomorrow was a day off. She didn't want to move another step today and had no plans to explore the city until the next morning after breakfast.

The square was now almost deserted. Juliet had taken off her shoes and socks, and pulled a second chair over to her table. She began tending to her aching feet with great concentration. With a small needle she popped the bulging blisters, and covered each with a plaster. Then she taped up her feet with white bandaging along the right and left sides and on her ankles. She took great care to ensure that there were no wrinkles in her socks and gently slipped her shoes back on. The salesperson had sold her the shoes a few weeks ago, assuring her that she wouldn't get blisters, even when walking a long distance in them. Wrong! It had started after just the first week of her hike: all of a sudden these vicious little things had flared up whilst walking, and they ached terribly. It took Juliet a while to find the right plasters at one of the pharmacies along her route; ones that weren't too thick but were still tough enough not to come loose after the first few metres. She had now become a master of dealing with blisters and gladly dispensed her advice to any fellow sufferers she met on the road who might be limping.

During her deep depression Juliet had come across a book describing the route she was now taking so powerfully and so vividly that she decided to grab this opportunity as her last hope. She was willing to try anything to find herself once more. Too long she had been teetering on the edge of the dark abyss; now she wanted to step towards the light.

Her flight to reach the starting point of her journey led straight into summer. The smiling sun alone seemed to lighten her spirit. With far much too much luggage on her shoulders, she started walking and after just two days sent half of her things back home from a small post office. Juliet began her route not in France, but in Spain. She didn't want to start climbing mountains right at the start and instead chose as her starting point the medieval city world-famous for its annual bull run. It took a whole afternoon for Juliet to find the small office where she could obtain a Credencial - her pilgrim pass. She had to cite the purpose of her journey and explain how she intended to cover the distance; on foot, on horseback or by bicycle. Juliet wrote, ‚For me, on foot.'

She quickly noticed that among the pilgrims there were many women with similar motives to hers. But very quickly all these sympathisers became too much, so she changed her daily routine. She no longer stayed in the typical pilgrim hostels and started her day later. At last she was alone with her own thoughts. To organise her thoughts and write down everything that seemed to be right and wrong with her former life, she kept a diary. The motto she wrote at the top of the first white sheet was an aphorism from Goethe: „You haven't really been somewhere unless you've been there on foot." And with each page she wrote, she felt a little lighter.

Juliet gazed once again at the magnificent cathedral; two doves rose up, circled in the air and landed high up on the left-hand corner tower. Juliet watched their flight, then stood up and entered the church through the mighty gates. She wanted to light another two candles; one for herself and one for Romeo.

Isolated Love

Bees buzzed around Juliet's head as she carefully opened the hive and took out the honeycomb. She was well protected so nothing could happen to her. She had situated the hives far above her old farmhouse in the middle of the shrubland which now in late spring was blooming in every colour. The multiple small huts that Juliet had painted herself in the style of her homeland stood on a mountain slope. The route down was arduous.

A shepherd with a grim visage and deep furrows on his sun-browned face had helped Juliet set up the beehives. In stark contrast to his appearance, he had a tender heart and tirelessly carried the wood up to her. Together they constructed the dwellings for Juliet's bee colonies, laughing and gesticulating the whole time. At first, they were only able to communicate with one another by gesture alone as the language the shepherd spoke was an incomprehensible mix of Italian and French. The inhabitants of the island were very proud of their land and their hard-won freedom. People would often spontaneously gather at the small inns in the villages to celebrate and sing their traditional Paghjellas.

Juliet climbed slowly down the little path, always being very careful that she didn't get caught in the rampant, thorny thicket of tangled shrubbery and wild roses. She loved the intense scent of broom, rosemary, thyme, lavender and sage. Everything was growing verdantly and with great diversity. For Juliet it was a joy to gather the herbs up and then use them later at home.

The goats were jumping up at her at the wooden fence at the bottom. The goats had finally given birth that week and Juliet urgently required the surplus of milk that the kids didn't need. She had become a remarkable cheese maker in recent years. The brocciu she produced with great care had achieved widespread acclaim. Among the farmers in the area, she was the only one who had not grown up there. Just a few years ago she had bought the old house for renovation and learned the tricky craft of cheese making with stoic calm and enduring zeal.

Her home was still an unfinished building site, but that did not bother her. Two rooms had been completed. In one there was a bed, in the other a large stove. Here she cooked, lived and worked. The ramshackle wooden shelves lining the windows stored all the products that Juliet had made herself: jars of honey, pure or mixed with different nuts, jams made of fruits from the garden, flavoured oils

and, of course, her brocciu at various stages of maturity. Juliet's preference was to eat the cheese when absolutely fresh, once it had been strained and sweetened with her own thyme honey. She could eat it by the spoonful.

Juliet lived quietly and avoided even going to the market to sell her products. She wanted to be completely alone. During the long period of her depression she had by chance read an article about this mountainous Mediterranean island which at that time distracted her from her own destructive thoughts. To find herself again, alone and without baggage; this was her only goal. She sold most of her possessions, leaving the rest behind, and arrived by ferry at the island with nothing but a small suitcase. The silence she longed for was what she had found in this house that nobody wanted, in a wild valley by the river.

The shepherd who had become a friend to Juliet came up to see her once a week and brought the things she needed. In return, she gave him the produce she had crafted during the week which he sold at market. She made a good living this way and for the first time she could remember, she really felt free. Sometimes Juliet was surprised at just how little she needed to be happy.

Infidelity

The hotel bar was a very famous place in this city. It had a charm very much of its own and was reminiscent of a typical American pub from the Prohibition era, even if it wasn't quite in the same league as the famous original on Rue Daunou in Paris.

Romeo was sitting roughly half-way down the bar itself with his back to the black piano on a small platform behind him. The pianist was very popular and it was clear he knew it, too. The bar was lively with no more room for further guests, and the clientèle crowded around the pianist. His rough, gentle voice had that special something that sends women into flights of fancy.

As always, the audience was very mixed. The uptight accountants from the offices opposite in their ill-fitting business suits who hadn't yet made it home were standing next to the hip and trendy folk who would be going on from here to the next club. Tourists and the simply curious who had come to the bar on guidebook recommendations rubbed shoulders with call girls who later on in the proceedings would help the bartender to get the hangers-on to take their leave.

Romeo was oblivious to all of this; his thoughts were still on the complicated negotiations with the Russian delegation who had come to this city to hear his business idea, an issue which was becoming increasingly confusing since the border had been opened. The two sides would only be able to reach an agreement with some painful compromise. He would have to agree to set up a subsidiary and even appoint a pro-government friend of the Russian client as Managing Director. Romeo had to give them his decision the next day. The pros and cons of this partnership circled incessantly in his head. He had the opportunity to gain a foot-hold in a new, interesting market, but he was also risking having to give up autonomy over his company, which he had always defended so fiercely.

It was a long, hard day that Romeo was allowing to fade away in the hubbub of the dancing crowd. His smartphone was showing thirteen missed calls. Instead of calling back, he ordered his fourth gin and tonic and dialled Juliet's number. He desperately needed to talk to her, wanted to hear her voice and take her advice, but yet again he only reached her voicemail. As so often, they were both travelling in their own worlds.

He stared ahead for a small eternity, and absently counted the backlit surfaces behind the bar. So at first he didn't notice the two blondes who were crowding in on him either side of his barstool. The first woman began the conversation by saying she was a first-time visitor to the city and was very excited. As far as Romeo could make out, the two were cousins. One came from the countryside, was married to her childhood sweetheart and had two children who were just about to leave school. The other had been living in the city for several years

and wanted to be an actress. Both came from a small town where the local language was pro-

nounced with a barking accent and rolled ‚r'.
Even the aspiring actress was unable to conceal
this dialect. That will limit the breadth of her
roles in the future, thought Romeo.

He was now on his tenth gin and tonic and awk-
wardly began to listen to more of their conversation. As her friend had to leave soon, the actress
leaned in conspiratorially to Romeo: after many
uneventful years of marriage, her cousin wanted to have a memorable experience; she asked
if understood what she meant, if he could help,
and if he had a room at the hotel.

Shortly thereafter, Romeo took the two blondes
up in the elevator to the top. The actress had
her hand in his trousers while her cousin was
still rather shy as Romeo opened her blouse
and felt her soft breasts.

Make a choice! Continue with ...
Remorse (p. 87) *or*
Love for Sale (p. 91)

Remorse

Romeo felt deeply ashamed. He had had a terrible day, and too much to drink, but it never should have happened. He went over his slip-up in his mind over and over, even though it was now almost six months ago.

The whole day he had been wandering around aimlessly in the city. First he strolled along the river, then climbed the almost 400 steps to the top of the massive cathedral and took in the breathtaking view of the Île de la Cité and the surrounding districts. Later he went back upstream on the shore, passing through narrow streets until he stood in front of the monumental iron lattice tower; the world-famous architectural icon that had come to symbolise the city. The queue of waiting visitors was way too long, so he went on to the Arc de Triomphe, almost got run over on the roundabout, and spent a long time gazing down the glamorous boulevard to the obelisk. He then climbed the famous staircase to the former artists' quarter in the north of the city. He had arranged to meet Juliet there, who had been at a conference that day.

Since the failed threesome in the hotel room, Romeo had been plagued by tremendous remorse. Although nothing significant had actually happened that night, he was ashamed of even attempting it. Romeo had been so drunk that despite the conscientious efforts of the two ladies, he was good for nothing. But he was not so drunk that he could no longer see what he was allowing himself to do. After the highly attractive cousins from the bar had removed their clothes, Romeo had decided to keep his eyes closed from that point on. He woke up the next morning alone in his bed; the maid had been knocking on the door for some time, and had finally mustered the courage to open the door.

Romeo really had to hurry so as not to miss his appointment with the Russian delegation. He explained politely but firmly that he wanted to move on from the joint venture option they had discussed the previous day. He didn't understand the Russian sentences that his business partners then switched to, but he certainly noticed that he had hit the outer limits of their enthusiasm and willingness to deal with him.

On his return flight, Romeo looked down at the cotton wool clouds below him, lost in thought.

He was glad to have not given away control of his company, but at the same time his thoughts were with Juliet constantly. She had changed in recent times; she had become more cautious in contrast to her old unbridled appetite for shopping and was working on her options to save their partnership. Romeo recognised her signals and he could see that she believed in a future with him. His mind wandered through all the wonderful memories they shared, and he jumped when the flight attendant offered him a drink and asked with concern if he was feeling OK. Romeo looked at her blankly; he hadn't noticed that tears were running down his cheek.

He was sitting in the old brasserie on the Place du Tertre where numerous cartoonists and painters were touting for business from the hordes of tourists. Beside him lay a bouquet of red roses. Romeo was highly agitated; he wanted to confide in Juliet about his infidelity, confirming to her the same time that he loved her with all his heart, and to ask for forgiveness.

Then he saw her, radiantly beautiful in her white dress as she entered the square from the direction of the Basilica. She seemed to float like an angel, stopped, brushed a strand of hair away from her face in an enchanting motion, and glanced in the direction of the bar where Romeo was waiting for her. He stood up and waved to her as their eyes met. A warm smile appeared on Juliet's face and Romeo knew that the two of them belonged together.

Love for Sale

Romeo's heart was racing, he was drunk and had taken some Tadalafil that he'd swallowed down with alcohol. To enhance the effect even more, he had put a ring on his erect penis, with another loop encircling his bulging testes. He lay on his back and was out of breath after several hours of exuberant sex. Amongst all the bodies writhing around on top of one another he had long lost track of what was going on. The companion he had found online for this evening had moved on from him after just a short time. He was sure she would be amusing herself on the lower floor of the spacious club.

Romeo turned onto his side and purveyed the scene. There were at least thirty naked bodies, wedging themselves into one another rhythmically in a dark room, indirectly illuminated with blue light. The monotonous moaning and panting from these people created a consistent noise level that was interrupted from time to time by ecstatic screams.

Directly in front of him was a brunette whose breasts were too big and too tight for her figure and her age. A dark-skinned, very muscular

man plunged his considerable manhood powerfully into her vagina while she was hard at work
satisfying two other men with her hands. The
whole situation looked altogether rather awkward, but for Romeo as a voyeur the scene was

extremely stimulating. From the back corner
of the room, two attractive women got up and
came over towards Romeo. Full of expectation,
he turned onto his back and closed his eyes.

It was already six clock in the morning as Romeo
got into a taxi in Liebenberggasse in the com-

pany of these two women. „What am I doing?",
Romeo asked himself, suddenly coming to his
senses. His desire to continue the orgy in the
hotel room had been extinguished all of a sudden when he observed ordinary life by the first
light of the dawn in this beautiful Art Nouveau
town. He told the taxi to stop, gave the driver a
large note and got out quickly. Disgusted with
himself, he turned off and disappeared down
the next street. He got lost on his way to the
castle garden and sat down on a bench. Romeo
knew that he was suffering from severe hyper-
sexuality that went far beyond simply an incre-
ased sexual desire for a woman. He was des-
perate; his relationship with Juliet was broken.
Weeping, he sat there and waited for the Palm
House to open. The season for the Heurigen,
the local young wine, had come early this year.

Make a choice! Continue with ...
Penitence (p. 94) *or*
Solitude (p. 99)

Penitence

Romeo had actually done it. Just as they used to, they set aside a weekend in their diaries and boarded the plane on Friday afternoon. They were staying in a very pleasant hotel on the Piazza d'Ognissanti, overlooking the river.

The next morning, after a hearty breakfast, they made their way into the city of the Medici. Numerous Renaissance masters had been immortalised here thanks to the support of their rich patrons, who in turn were satisfying their own vanity. In perfect weather they strolled along the river bank in the direction of the historical centre, with its charming streets and squares. At last, they stood in front of the old segmental arch bridge lined on both sides with rows of small businesses, previously owned exclusively by butchers and tanners. These days all you could find there were shops for tourists with souvenirs and jewellery, and hordes of people. They continued on to the Piazza della Signoria, where Romeo insisted on drinking an espresso in the café on the corner and wanted to try the homemade chocolate.

In the evening they met Riccardo, the establishment's sommelier responsible for purchasing, and they visited the enoteca's gigantic wine cellar. Riccardo was an old friend of Romeo's who took the opportunity to guide them personally through the hallowed halls. As far as the eye could see, wine bottles of many different vintages with handwritten labels citing the best locations and famous wineries were stored on wooden shelves. The cellar was indeed breathtaking, especially of course for people who like to drink wine.

The owner of this excellent restaurant was himself a great wine lover who had helped out his local colleagues more than once when they needed a special bottle of wine for their establishments.

Even among the Cantinetta of the largest wine producers in the city, he was the go-to person whenever anyone needed a rare label or two to satisfy a promise to a good customer which they couldn't fulfil themselves.

It had taken a lot for Romeo and Juliet to be able to go travelling together like this after the events of the past few years. It was not easy for Romeo to find the right therapist whom he could trust. But when he finally began therapy, this turned out to be the key to his recovery. Romeo delved painstakingly into his own self-image, he was noticeably more at peace, had slowed down the pace of his life and even allowed himself to be persuaded to spend a week in a silent monastery for a period of solitude. This journey to find himself was exceptionally healing for Romeo. He returned a whole different person, started playing sports again, reduced his alcohol consumption and had found new joy in life.

„How could I have been so blind, why did it take me so long to realise?" he asked Theo, tears in his eyes. For over six months he had attended these sessions three times a week, relaxing and breathing deeply with his therapist and mentor, when Theo mooted the idea of joint sessions with Juliet. Romeo jumped up in panic, but Theo reassured him in his caring, understanding way, and finally he agreed.

The conversations with Juliet in Theo's practice were initially awkward and faltering, but as early as the third meeting they were both able to laugh about the old times. After the fourth session, they parted company with a peck on the cheek and three months later they were planning this week-end together, albeit under supervision.

After a day full of wonderful memories, they were now sitting in the elegant restaurant at Via Ghibellina and enjoying the tasting menu where the chef impressively demonstrated his skills, accompanied by excellent wines which Riccardo had carefully selected. It was a lovely evening, but it was getting late and Romeo wanted to leave. He settled the bill secretly on his way to the bathroom.

Back at the table, the pair warmly took their leave from Juliet and her new partner. Romeo took Theo's hand and they walked through the balmy evening back to the hotel. The next morning they wanted to be at the Galleria dell' Accademia as early as possible to view the well-proportioned figure of David, the statue of all statues. Juliet looked at the pair of them pensively, but with a smile following on her lips. „Life is beautiful", she wanted to shout to Romeo, „enjoy it, because it is very short".

Solitude

Romeo lived almost exclusively off soup or porridge. After losing all his incisors down to the rotting stumps and with the remaining molars receding far from the gums at the root crowns, every bite was painful. With enough alcohol, he was even able to make droll comments about his situation. To his new friends who had recently saved his life from a perilous situation, he explained – without teeth but with heart – that he would be unlikely to be able to accept any dinner invitations for the better part of that year. And he had certainly never been much of a cook anyway, so his teeth were no great loss after all.

As a result of his years of excess in the red-light district, Romeo increasingly lost his grip on his former life. After Juliet left him, his friends followed suite, and his company was soon passed into the hands of the administrators who made every attempt to avoid bankruptcy.

He became more and more unkempt, and let himself go. Brushing his teeth once a week would have to be enough, and only then if he was able to find some toothpaste from some dustbin or other on his wanderings through the city. He was pleased that not everyone squeezed out every single scrap of toothpaste from the tube or even cut it open to scrape out the final little bit. In fact, he was convinced that very few people in this high-speed society gave any thought to leaving anything behind for the

poor guys who had hit rock bottom. He was not thinking in particular about money from the state; instead, in his confused head he had concocted his own pragmatic approach. They could all live in the land of plenty, he explained to his shivering homeless friends, if every citizen were to give away just 10 to 20 percent of non-consumed food to people like them.

His plan to establish a high class brothel specifically for managers of large companies, government officials or consulate and embassy staff with some prostitutes did not fail due to lack of demand, but due to the pimps who were very forceful in registering their ownership of the ladies. Romeo, who was completely inexperienced in the field of high-class prostitution, hadn't reckoned on the vehemence with which these gents would drive their point home.

As a former high-flying businessman he tried his usual approach for reaching a compromise acceptable to both parties. „Let's talk first about the pros and cons of a partnership", he started to say. The overly well-built men with their square, hairless heads did not even have the decency to respond to this proposal, however. A fleshy, but very well-practised fist slammed into Romeo's face with such a force that – fortunately – he immediately lost consciousness. Fists and boots flew without mercy at his body lying on the ground. Had his new friends not happened to notice the attack and get help, Romeo would certainly have departed this life once and for all that day.

He hadn't been a part of everyday life for some time now; he didn't read the newspapers and didn't listen to any news. On the contrary, he wanted to forget and hide away from reality. In order to sleep, he dulled his sense of shame and the constantly freezing temperatures with cheap alcohol. He generally then went to the English Garden, the large park in the heart of the city. He would sit on a bench on the bank of Eisbach river near the art museum where the rapids formed that wave popular with surfers from all over the world. The evening was unusually mild for the time of year, a warm foehn wind from the Alps gusted over the city.

Romeo was tired of the daily struggle to find warm places to sleep and cheap red wine. Even among the lower orders of society there were uncompromising rules and set hierarchies. He lay down on the park bench and fell into a dreamless sleep. The warnings of the severe hurricane storm had passed him by; it was now sweeping south across the country at over 140 kilometres an hour, driving sharp ice crystals through the air ahead of it. The storm reached the city at midnight. Romeo was fast asleep and did not feel a thing. He was found the next morning by the hardcore surfers who were riding the waves even at this time of year.

To my team

Thank you to Amy Bradley and Chantal de Mür for their tireless patience, enthusiasm and attentiveness in handling the many tasks involved in getting the book finalised and printed.

Thank you to Hans-Joachim Ellerbrock for the many conversations discussing – albeit not ultimately resolving – the question of „what holds the inner workings of the world together". Thank you for the valuable advice and design work.

Thank you to Sandra Stoller, who with her winning ways and personable manner was able to keep everything running smoothly at all times between all parties, and coordinate the timings despite the tight schedule.

Thank you to Dr. Andreas Klement for his calm, professional and constructive support as editor and advisor. His obvious enthusiasm for the concept of the book and its realisation was greatly appreciated.

Christian Zott